POKY
and Friends™
The Truth About Kittens & Puppies

Adapted by Naomi Kleinberg from a script by Bruce Talkington

Illustrated by DRi Artworks   Cover painted by Don Williams

🐦 A GOLDEN BOOK • NEW YORK

Golden Books Publishing Company, Inc., New York, New York 10106

One sunny day the Poky Little Puppy was playing in the backyard with his brothers Pip, Pickle, and Pug, and their sister, Pattycake. Pug had heard some exciting news.

"The funniest looking dog I've ever seen has moved into the Feldmans' barn," Pug told the others.

"He's funny looking because he's a cat, silly!"
Pattycake explained with a giggle.

"Cats have yellow eyes that can see in the dark!" Pip
said in a loud whisper, opening his own eyes wide.

"And they've got sharp claws that pop in and out!" Pattycake added as she tried to do the same.

"Yeah," Pickle said breathlessly, "and lots of extra lives. Something big, like three or twenty-six!"

"Nine, Pickle," Pattycake told him. "A cat has nine lives."

"That's because they always land on their feet when they fall!" Pug said as he tried to scratch his ear—but fell over instead.

"Well," said Poky, all excited, "with so many differences between cats and dogs, it's going to be fun getting to know this cat!"

Later that day Poky decided to take a look around the barn. Suddenly he found himself face-to-face with a furry stranger.

"Yikes!" Poky yelled in fright. He turned and ran the other way!

"Yeow!" screeched the stranger diving behind a bucket.

After a moment Poky carefully peeked out of his hiding place.

"Who are you?" he and the stranger asked at the same time.

"I asked you first!" said Poky.

"I'm Shy," the other replied.

"My name is Poky. Say," he whispered, "have you seen a cat around here?"

"A cat?" Shy whispered in return. "What's that? How would I be able to tell?"

"Cats have big yellow eyes that can see in the dark," Poky explained as he checked around the barn.

"Like these?" asked Shy, opening her yellow eyes very wide.

Poky looked carefully at her eyes. "Gee, no. A cat's eyes would be scarier than that."

Poky kept looking around the barn for the cat. "And cats have nasty looking claws," he went on.

Shy spread her claws and tapped Poky gently on the back. "Hey, Shy," Poky yelped. "What did you do that for?"

"So, what else do you know about cats?" Shy asked Poky.
"They always land on their feet," he replied.
With that, Shy dove off a hay bale, twisted around in midair, and landed gently on her feet right next to Poky.

Poky stared at Shy. Suddenly they both began to giggle.
"You're him!" Poky declared. "You're the cat!"
"Yes, but I'm HER. And I'm a *kitten*," Shy said firmly,
and laughed some more.

"Well, what else can kittens do?" Poky asked Shy as
they took a walk around the farm.

In answer, Shy raced up the trunk of the nearest tree.
"We can climb trees really fast—watch this!" she replied.

"Puppies dig holes really fast," Poky bragged as he furiously shoveled dirt with his paws.

Shy came down to look into the hole.

"And you get dirty really fast, too," she said, shaking some dirt off her fur.

"That's the best part!" Poky said happily.

The two wandered through a flowerbed and across the yard.
"Kittens love to play with yarn," Shy explained as they
reached the back porch of the Feldmans' farmhouse. She
nudged a ball of yarn out of the knitting basket and batted
it around.

"A ball!" Poky growled happily, chasing after the yarn. In no time, he'd gotten himself completely tangled in it. "This is fun!" he said to his new friend.

Shy explained to Poky that kittens also liked to play with mice. She took Poky back to the barn to show him where mice could be found. The two of them waited patiently.

"Hi, Mischa," purred Shy when a mouse finally came out of the hole.

"Uh, oh!" the little fellow sighed as Shy slipped her paw under him. Shy then tossed Mischa up in the air, caught him, and threw him up again and again. Head over heels Mischa went, just like a circus acrobat.

Suddenly Poky jumped in and grabbed Mischa by the tail. "Hey, careful, Poky!" Mischa squeaked. "I need my tail!"

"What are you doing, you silly puppy?" Shy asked in surprise.

"I was afraid he'd get hurt," Poky explained.

"But that's what kittens and mice do!" answered Shy with a little frown.

"Look, Shy," Poky said. "You're a kitten and I'm a puppy, and I don't chase you or growl at you. Why do you have to be that way with Mischa? Can't we all be friends?"

Mischa and Shy looked at each other in surprise.

The kitten thought for a moment. "Do you think we could be friends?" she asked the mouse.

Mischa didn't answer.

"Come on, Mischa," Poky urged. "If I can do it and she can do it, you can do it, too."

Mischa spoke slowly. "Well, maybe I could," he said at last.

"Great!" Poky said happily.

So Poky, Shy, and Mischa discovered that the world can be full of friends. And that's important, because after a whole day filled with running and jumping and playing, having a friend means there will always be someone there for you to lean on.